For Scout and Finn, who make a big splash wherever they go.
And for Pete, who asked for co-author credit.

VIKING

An imprint of Penguin Random House LLC, New York

First published in the United States of America by Viking,

an imprint of Penguin Random House LLC, 2020

Text and illustrations copyright © 2020 by Abi Cushman

Visit us online at penguinrandomhouse.com

LIBRARY OF CONGRESS CATALOGING-IN-PUBLICATION DATA IS AVAILABLE

ISBN 9781984836625

Manufactured in China

Book design by Abi Cushman and Jim Hoover

Art drawn in pencil and colored digitally

1   3   5   7   9   10   8   6   4   2

SOAKED!

Abi Cushman

VIKING

Look at all this rain.
Everything is **dreary**.
Everything is **drenched**.
And no one is happy.

Not that badger.

Not that bunny.

Because the rain ruins **everything**.

Ice cream cones.

Sandcastles.

Cashmere sweaters.

All the things that
bears **love**.

What's that you say?

Why don't we just
go inside my cave
until the rain stops?

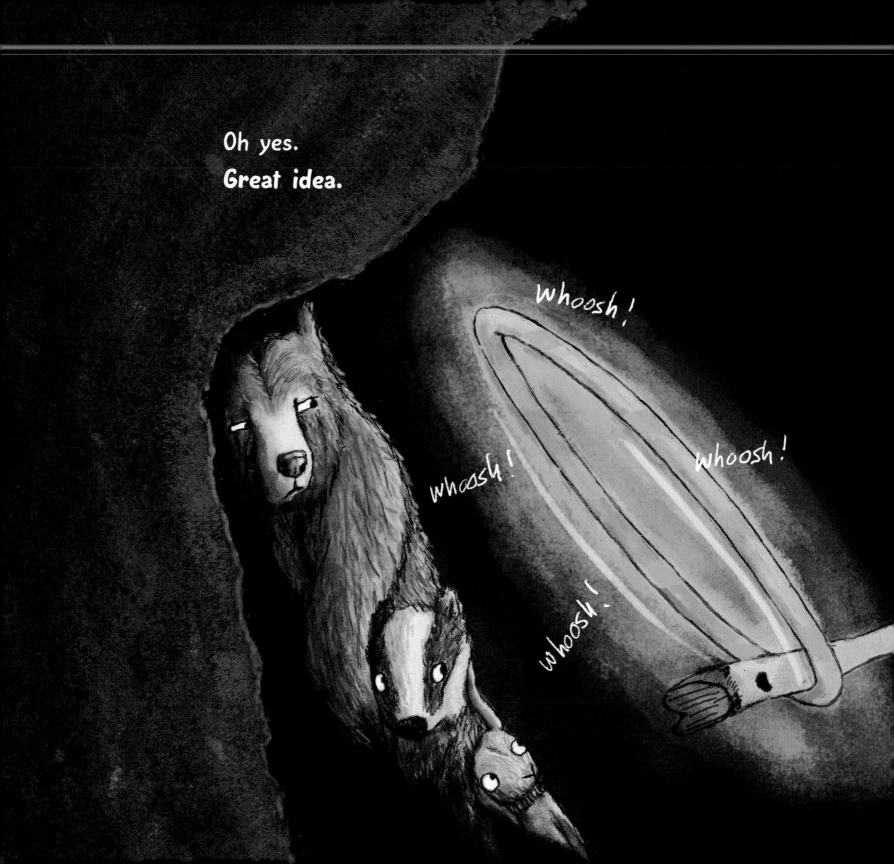

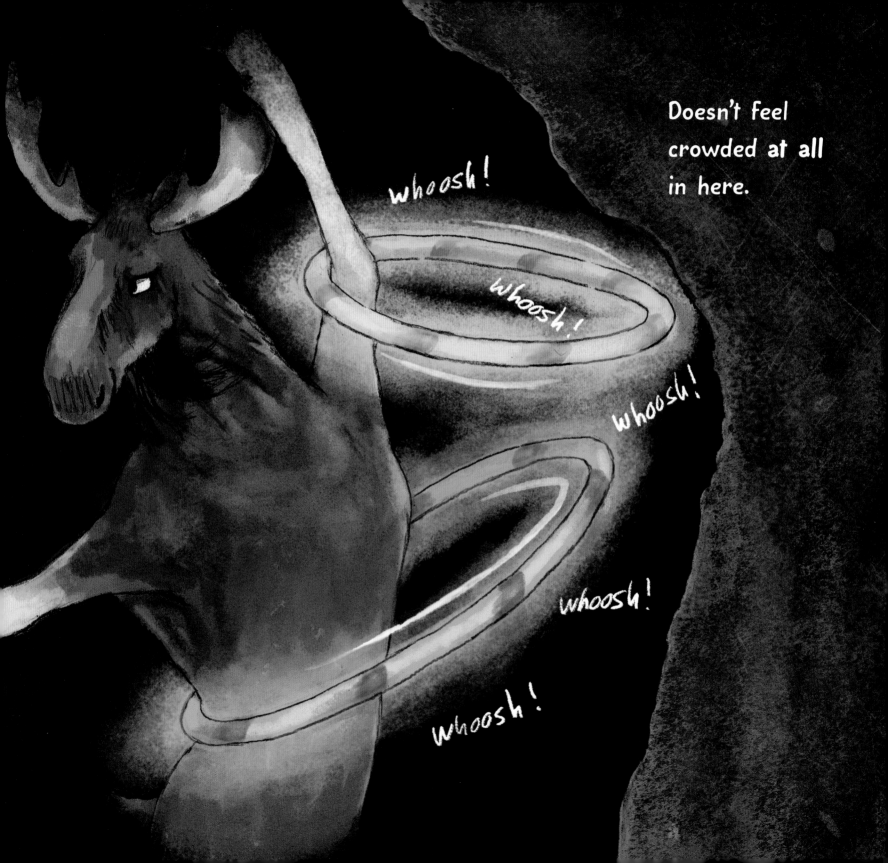

And sure, I'd love to use my umbrella.

FWOOP!

The blue one with the bumblebees on it.

But everyone looked, and no one can find it.

Badger said she found **her**
blue bumblebee umbrella.

But not mine.

Blah.

I guess I'll just
go sit on my log
and wallow.

Wait a minute.
We can't have a Hula-Hooping moose
without a Hula-Hoop, can we.

Great. We got it.
Now I can return to
wallowing on my—

Me? Try the Hula-Hoop?

SERIOUSLY?
Oh okay, fine!
But I won't
have any fun.

There. I did it. Totally
unfun. Just like I thought.
Now if you'll excuse me,
I need a moment to myself.

Look at all this rain.
Everyone is splashing!

And it's so **splishy** and **sploshy!**

Silly and **soggy!**

It's so—

Oh.
Did the rain stop?

Blah.

Too sunny.

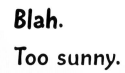